And I Have To Pay For The F*cking Flowers?

A heads up for the Father of the Bride on how you are about to get really screwed.

(And a few things you can do about it.)

Jay H. Heyman

Jay H. Heyman

Copyright © 2018 Jay H. Heyman

All rights reserved. This book or any portion thereof may not be reproduced or used in any manner whatsoever without the express written permission of the author except for the use of brief quotations in a book review.

COVER DESIGN: Jeffrey Felmus
AUTHOR PHOTOGRAPH: Christopher Duggan

And I Have to Pay for the F*cking Flowers?

NOTE:

As the Father of the Bride (FOB) there are two ways your wallet will be flattened. One is that just as fish eggs become exorbitantly expensive when they are labeled "caviar," so too does any expense go through the ceiling, if it is used in the same sentence as the word "wedding."

Also, you are traditionally expected to pay for certain expenses. However, the groom's family can be expected to attempt to move as many of the total wedding costs as possible to your side of the ledger. This does not mean they are all cheap bastards. But this guide assumes that they are. And I do not hear you disagreeing.

Jay H. Heyman

Table of Contents

Goats and Handshakes. 7

Certainly you should pay thousands for a photographer. (Because one guest may not have a smart phone with a camera.)..12

Your liquor must all be top shelf—apparently bending down for a bottle is just not done..17

Your computer has over ninety different fonts. So of course you will pay someone else to create the invitations........................22

Why does one DJ cost more than actual live musicians? 28

This is where you rehearse paying for more stuff. 32

A wedding planner is like a financial planner. But with the exact opposite goal. 36

And I Have to Pay for the F*cking Flowers?

When your guests can't eat another bite, it's time to serve them dinner. 40

A penguin is an expensive role model. 46

You will lose twenty pounds. Mostly from your wallet. 49

The Cake. It's spelled "tiers," but it's pronounced "tears." 53

No matter what your favorite flowers are, they will be out of season. 56

Incidentally, it never ends. 59

The venue. So many variables. So much money. 65

Help! There are so many of "them," and only one of me. 68

Have you noticed a theme here?............71

OK, I know the groom goes through some shit too. 75

The good news. 79

Jay H. Heyman

About The Author 80

And I Have to Pay for the F*cking Flowers?

Goats and Handshakes.

There was a time, known as the good old days, when if your daughter were to get married, there would be goats given and handshakes exchanged. And that was that. *

Today, everyone involved with producing a wedding has the unspoken but heartfelt desire to transfer as large a portion of his or her student debt to your bank account. They do it with a pricing structure more appropriate to a seven turret moated castle than a wedding hall.

Yes, the rules have changed. And we know who has changed the rules, has altered the previously accepted monetary customs, and has realigned the financial responsibilities of each party. We know it is not you, the father of the bride. Actually, you have done everything short of purchasing a ladder to suggest that eloping is not merely a movie cliché, but rather an honored tradition. No, it is the family of the groom that holds fast to the tradition that only the father of the bride should feel the pain (they call it the "joy") of learning the ins and outs of Chapter 11 bankruptcy.

You will discover that your future son-in-law, who is not yet really a relative, but rather remains a relative stranger — a person that you are not even certain of his middle name, let alone what he actually does for a living — will always side with his family. He truly thinks it is absolutely reasonable that you alone should bankroll the pomp and ceremony that makes it all legal and permissible for him to continue bedding your own flesh and blood.

And I Have to Pay for the F*cking Flowers?

Anyway, don't think that praying for some kind of equitable solution will produce any positive results. For no matter which God you speak to, these all-powerful beings believe that the fancier the ceremony, the more they are glorified. They also prefer — because many of the gods, while great at miracles, are barely adequate in math — that one person (the FOB) should foot the wedding bill, rather than dividing the cost like separate checks at Miss America diner.

Still, don't think that any one religion has discovered the secret to minimizing expenses. For a Jewish ceremony you will discover that Kosher translates as "We will charge you for smoked salmon, but we will be serving lox." In traditional Hindu and Baraat weddings — in which the ceremony often lasts longer than many marriages — you will pay huge sums to rent elephants and horses, with their attendant costumes and attendant attendants. For Catholics, the additional costs are associated with the copious amounts of alcohol consumed, often followed by the expenditure for the EMS ambulances. Protestants, Baptists, and even agnostics have costs associated with their particular unique ceremonies; I just don't know enough about them to be disparaging.

Furthermore, don't count on your daughter to intervene on your behalf. Part of the reason why she will allow your wallet to be trampled is that she is proud that you can afford to be so generous, intentionally or otherwise. The other element is her realization that the more that "you" pay for, the less "they" pay for, and since she is becoming part of "they," this leaves more money available for her honeymoon.

This guide is designed to create some fairness to the monetary expectations of each participating member of the wedding party. Leave it lying around where the family of the groom — the family that will knock back all your champagne, wolf all your food, and then try to acquire every table's flower arrangement — can see it. Perhaps it will help. But at the very least, perhaps they then may be willing to co-sign the loan you took to cover it all.

*Nowadays, weddings are not only between a man and a woman. There are more potential combinations than there are varieties of martinis: Gay, lesbian, transgender, mixed, and religious, to name a few. But I don't have the strength to include all the possibilities. I will simply use bride and groom to symbolize any two people who have chosen to wed. So when I use "Him," or "Her," be aware that I also mean "them," "it," "both," "trollop," "Pat easy lay," and "dumpling."

Jay H. Heyman

Certainly you should pay thousands for a photographer. (Because one guest may not have a smart phone with a camera.)

Ahhh, golden memories. They are wonderful things. But you will soon find out why they are known as "golden" memories. As you may dimly recall, there was a time when cameras used something called "film." It was usually 35mm, and came in rolls of 36 pictures. Between the price of the camera, the expense of the film and the cost of developing the pictures, it was quite expensive. When you added up all the costs, it made economic sense to indulge in a professional to take the wedding pictures.

Then came disposable cameras, placed on each table. More often than not, you ended up with close-ups of cuff links, nostrils and the bride's elbow, but it was a reasonable budgetary solution.

Today, virtually everyone has a phone that can take hundreds of hi-res digital images, from selfies to panoramas to portrait mode. And just as an infinite number of monkeys and a keyboard can outdo Shakespeare, any ten inebriated guests can completely document every second of the entire ceremony, with more than enough first-rate results to fill a photo book thick enough for you to use as your gym weight workout.

Since you, the FOB, are the one opening your wallet, nothing less than a paid professional is acceptable. But first, you will spend (waste) hours selecting the perfect photographer. You will look at the pictures from previous weddings they have shot. (Perhaps not the best verb to describe their activities.) You will quickly see that photos of one wedding and another wedding are pretty much interchangeable.

There are the adoring couple, the compulsory black and whites, the posed, the casuals, the families, the friends, the future mother-in-law who always manages to close her eyes, and the cousin who looks as if he has a serious neck injury, thanks to always sticking his head forward in the belief it will hide a few of his many chins.

And when you ask for your daughter's input as to the style, range and creativity of a particular photographer, the comments you get will be along the lines of, "I didn't like her dress" "Who let her wear that color

And I Have to Pay for the F*cking Flowers?

lipstick?" "Is that a tattoo or a birthmark?" In other words, no help at all.

Again, it truly won't make a difference. No matter the amount of money "they" will shame you into spending for these life-long memories, you will get the same results Rachel gets with her new fairly smart phone.

Did I mention the photo booth? It is usually placed in the most inaccessible space possible, since having one embarrasses even the bride and groom. And it can only be discovered by following the trail of yellow feathers that have fallen off the feathered boas that are part of the array of props that (surprise) you have paid for. Why do well-attired guests want to have nonsensical photos of themselves, accessorized in oversized sunglasses, leis, and red velvet hats — which are some of the more understated props — as souvenirs of the event? Just check out the last four words of the earlier sentence. The words that read: "you have paid for."

You will end up with a minimum of one photographer, an assistant, and the videographer, whether you really want them all or not. And you will marvel at the photographer's supernatural ability of focusing on the third cousin you don't really know, and whom you invited only because she lives so far away you never believed she would accept the invitation. But she will be in the center of more pictures than the bride's sister.

*And I Have to Pay for the F*cking Flowers?*

Your liquor must all be top shelf—apparently bending down for a bottle is just not done.

It seems that the 5-liter, boxed, plastic cup crowd would be insulted if you didn't serve the finest vintage wines in all available hues (red, white, rosé) and textures (bubbles, fizzy, sparkling, still, *petillant*). And the bubbly served has to be from the actual Champagne area, not the ordinary Prosecco that we all delightedly drink on a daily basis.

After all, if the wedding toast glass is filled with anything less than vintage Dom Perignon, the marriage is of course doomed. As is your credit rating.

Jay H. Heyman

There must be more available options for alcohol than there are grains of rice tossed after the ceremony. Not just the usual booze, but also a variety of distilled grains that few knew were still in existence. Uncle Harry must have his Canadian Club, Bonita her Four Roses. Though each will have one drink, promptly take a nap, and sleepily miss most of the rest of the festivities.

Keep in mind, also, that no matter how much alcohol you order, it will not be enough. This is because your guests know they have already heavily invested in wedding presents, so even the teetotalers will seek to get some of their outlay back in alcohol consumption.

(Though it is a cliché, it is true that this is one area that does really reduce costs for a Jewish wedding. One bottle of Manischewitz per table of ten is more than sufficient for the evening.)

And I Have to Pay for the F*cking Flowers?

The distressing monetary news is that you will be supplying the before, during, and after liquid refreshments.

BEFORE: To calm their nerves, every member of the wedding party, and most of the guests, will have a pre-ceremony shot. Or two. There is probably no higher amount of liquor-to-price ratio than a shot. Considering the bar can get at a minimum of 25 shots out of a bottle, and the least you will be charged is five bucks a shot, you are in for over one hundred dollars per bottle.

DURING: This is almost too depressing to discuss. The liquid refreshment will keep flowing like the Danube, to make up for the drying up of conversations. Guests seated together at a table—based on some well-intentioned but never successful seating plan—soon realize they have little to talk about. And since it is difficult to talk behind someone's back when they are sitting next to you, even whispering is soon suspended. Again, since it is your wallet that is involved, not theirs, you will probably be shamed into paying the additional premium to have wine poured tableside, to accommodate guests who are too drunk to make it the five feet to the nearest bar.

AFTER: It is not the Irish coffees that will hurt you financially. It is not even the obscure retro after-dinner liqueurs, like Grand Marnier and Chartreuse that millennials will suddenly crave as proof of their maturity. No, what will make the deepest holes in your wallet are the drinks that people have heard of, but never had the chance to experience. Till now, when you are buying the next, and every, round. So thanks to you, there will be an outpouring — literally — of White Russians, Vodka Stingers, Grasshoppers, Brandy Alexanders,

And I Have to Pay for the F*cking Flowers?

and depending upon the political climate, Cuba Libres.

No matter how complete you think the above list is, you will soon find out that you have omitted another costly necessity: The Signature Drink. This is the beverage that is devised by the wedding couple, and either in name or ingredients honors some obscure moment in their past. And it will never be Scotch on the rocks, even if they were born in Scotland, met in Scotland, or are planning to honeymoon in Scotland. No, the ingredients will read like a list of rare metals. Such as one part Absinthe, two parts '47 Richebourg, one part gold. (No, not Goldwasser liqueur. Actual gold.)

Jay H. Heyman

Your computer has over ninety different fonts. So of course you will pay someone else to create the invitations.

At the end of the movie *The Wizard Of Oz*, the wizard tells the lion that he always had the same courage as everyone else, but he was lacking one thing: A medal. Well, you will find that no matter how perfect your handwriting and graphic design computer skills, you will be missing one important talent: Calligraphy. Calligraphy is the extraordinary ability to turn a mere 26 letters into a major source of revenue.

People judge a calligrapher's skill by how fancy they can make each word, using

And I Have to Pay for the F*cking Flowers?

closed loops and open swirls, with the highest praise going to how close to a doctor's handwriting they can get. And the murmuring you hear is not understated appreciation of the final result. It is more along the lines of, "Is that an 'e' or an 'a'"?

The first thing you are on the hook for are the "Save the date" cards. Now, how many people do you know whose social calendar is so packed that they need six months notice for an event?

Truth is, the "Save the Date" cards are not really about saving a date. They are code for "Look who finally caught a guy." Basically, bragging rights that you are paying for. And since it comes so early in the ritual, you will make the classic rookie mistake. "Oh, it's just a card. How much can that cost?"

Well, let me throw a few words out at you: Vellum, Intaglio, letterpress, process, spot varnish, gloss, uncoated, silk.... And those are just your choices of what variety of paper the card will be printed on.

These cards will be your first excursion into the wedding choice jungle. And you will quickly discover that since again, it is you, the FOB who will be paying, the choices decided upon are rarely related to which looks the best. It is just assumed (by "them") that whatever is the most expensive has to be the highest quality.

Then it gets better (worse). Because before you can select a printer, designer, engraver, you have to make "The List." Actually, there is never such thing as a list. You will have to create a "spreadsheet." Which is another time intensive talent you will have to acquire. You will discover there is the "A" list, the "B" list and often the "C" list. And while this doesn't directly add to the cost, the cliché that time is money is very

And I Have to Pay for the F*cking Flowers?

true. So you will be diverting your attention from your job, your spouse, and your hobbies, to focus on this often once in a lifetime event. It will cost you in many non-financial ways, but it will indeed cost you.

Happily, you will be getting a valuable education in typography and design. And the way you will know it is valuable is because the education will end up costing you about as much as a two-year college. But you will soon be rattling off terms like serif, non-serif, leading and kerning like a pro. It is a wonderful skill to acquire, though one that you will never have need of again.

As with many of the choices you will be making, there will be a large number of potential printers that you will find online. Miraculously, each will have a 5 star rating, nothing but favorable comments, and a web site more appealing than many of the venues you are exploring. But using an online resource is like telling people that your daughter and her future husband met on an online dating site. There's nothing wrong with that, but somehow it irks.

So you will visit the offices of real printers, and look at book after book of invitations, trying discreetly to break the cost code. Is BV56 more expensive than VB76? How much more expensive will the postage be if the envelope is lined with gold foil?

At some point, determined more by the calendar than the actual talent of a printer, you will decide on the invitation, the RSVP piece, the hotel information, the rehearsal dinner address, and the little extras that somehow also have to be stuffed into the envelope (confetti, sparkles, ribbons). This insures that not only will you have all those without a good quality vacuum cleaner curse

And I Have to Pay for the F*cking Flowers?

your confetti, but also that you will be paying the highest possible postage rate.

Jay H. Heyman

Why does one DJ cost more than actual live musicians?

Though there are many vows exchanged on the wedding day, there is never a vow of silence. In fact, there is the unspoken pledge to make that day the nosiest possible, as if sheer volume will guarantee blissful memories. So when you suggest music that is modern and tasteful, like a guitarist, or a harpist, "they" will suggest you have your head up your ass. Which is never a good way to listen to music.

Of course the music selections are dependent upon the culture, the ages of the bride and groom, the venue, and so on. The most important factor is that the DJ must supply his or her own drugs. Actually, the most important factor seems to be that the DJ must have had his hearing impaired during previous engagements, so that the softest he can play and actually hear his own sound is at level 9.

As you will do with most of the people you select for the wedding, you must check credentials and obtain references. The musician will supply a sample CD, which he could have purchased on the street, or borrowed from a talented friend. So there is nothing for you to do but actually go to an event where he will be the DJ. And while all oversampled music sounds pretty much alike, you will have to make a decision. Though you will try to make a reasonable choice, based on price, availability and sound, your daughter, who has the final say, will inevitably pick the DJ who has the tattoo of Adele on his arm. Of course, he will be the most expensive, since he is accumulating money to pay for the laser removal of the tattoo.

One reason for the outrageous musical expense is that no matter what format the DJ requires the music to be in, it will be incompatible with whatever format you have, and will have to be re-formatted. And I am not talking an obsolete 8-track here. Your mp3 will not work with his CD collection, and his vinyl will not work with your tapes. Which is why, when he plays the music to accompany the magic first dance with your daughter, his struggles to play your requested choice guarantees that you will not recognize the song you spent months carefully selecting.

Part of the problem, to be candid, is not just the expense. It is the wide range of ages of the guests. For example, the parents of the marriage couple, and the friends of the

And I Have to Pay for the F*cking Flowers?

parents, might have grown up when the most risqué lyric suggested that two people spend the night together. Yet the friends of the bride and groom are probably listening to songs with lyrics that make the title of this guide seem as tame as a children's book.

And each age group wants to hear the music they are most comfortable dancing to, be it the waltz, swing, line dancing, electronic, or salsa. So even if you have hired the most expensive DJ, the majority of the music he plays will be disliked by most of the guests, most of the time, since he is not playing their kind of music. But as the event wears down, with just a few guests still standing, and even fewer still swaying, you will only have one question: How much extra do I have to pay to never hear the Macarena again?

Jay H. Heyman

This is where you rehearse paying for more stuff.

This particular expense has many names, the most common being "The Rehearsal Dinner." But all that is actually rehearsed that evening is how to drink to excess and eat too much, with which we have all had a lifetime of practice, and will be duplicating the following day.

Members of the wedding party, and seemingly randomly selected others, are invited to attend this event, since the fear is that they will not see enough of each other throughout the next 24 hours.

And I Have to Pay for the F*cking Flowers?

Your first choice, no matter what it is, will be wrong, and more expensive. I am talking about the dreaded "Open Bar." The word that has been omitted over time is "wallet," as in "Open Wallet Bar."

Basically, your two choices are an open bar, where you pay one (enormous) set price for unlimited beverages during the cocktail hour. Or you can choose to pay for each drink. And it doesn't matter if you are a CPA or math professor, your odds of guessing correctly are worse than playing the slots on a cruise ship. Remember, the venue has played this game many times over; you are doing it for the first time.

Let's say you select paying for each individual drink. That is the venue's clue to delay the actual serving of any food as long as they can, to keep the cocktail hour going as long as possible. And each server is trained to be so solicitous, inquiring if anyone would like another drink, even if the glasses in front of guests have not yet even been lifted.

However, if you select the option of paying one set price for unlimited drinks, they will have you in and out of the bar area faster than you can clamp on a clip-on bowtie.

The rehearsal dinner is where all the people who will be criticizing your FOB speech the next day will be giving their own talks. And each will end with an actual toast, which is never saluted with a sip of soda. No, each toast must be accompanied by an expensive glass of champagne, a tradition that began in the rocky soil of the Champagne region of France, as they tried to figure out how to unload their bubbly version of tart white wine. And they succeeded in convincing the world that these bubbles are a good thing, though it actually makes as much sense as serving flat Coca-Cola, or carbonated coffee.

Jay H. Heyman

A wedding planner is like a financial planner. But with the exact opposite goal.

Financial planners do their best to invest your money wisely, hoping that they can help your resources grow. Ideally, you have carefully selected and vetted the financial planner you work with, enjoying the benefit of a long-term relationship, and clearly stated goals.

This is as opposed to a wedding planner, whom you have selected in a panicky rush at the last possible moment, since you never thought you were going to need one till "they" said you couldn't do it yourself. When

And I Have to Pay for the F*cking Flowers?

you pointed out that you have run your own business, raised a family, planned vacations, selected schools and purchased houses, how difficult can a six hour wedding be, their one word answer is "very."

The first thing you will do when you select the wedding planner is to tell her your budget. The second thing you will do is double that amount, if only to stop her from choking to death from the force of her laughter. When you point out that basically you are talking about two people walking down an aisle, standing in front of a clergyperson, and reciting a few vows, her laughter will only intensify.

What kinds of planning can you expect the wedding planner to bring to the party to justify what you will be paying? For the most part, nothing you would ever notice, or care about. "Oh look," no one will say, "the bride's nail polish matches the napkins."

And, "Isn't it amazing that if you were able to look down from the ceiling, and if the chandelier wasn't there, the tables would appear to form a practically perfect star."

The paradox is that planning, by definition, takes time. But since no matter when you start, you are immediately way behind schedule, you will learn a language you thought only existed in movies featuring labor unions: double time, golden time, overtime, premium and time and a half.

A wedding planner can help you find a venue, a caterer, make-up people, DJs, photographers and anything else you might need. They will also help you discover the differences among a secured loan, a second mortgage and prime plus two.

There is a saying that men plan and God laughs. And God never laughs harder than

And I Have to Pay for the F*cking Flowers?

when he hears the plans of a wedding planner.

Jay H. Heyman

When your guests can't eat another bite, it's time to serve them dinner.

A menu was once known as a "Bill of Fare." But you will soon discover that there is little that is "Fare" about it for a wedding. When you attended other events, the magic words announcing dinner was about to be served were "Everyone, please go to your assigned table."

But the way your guests will know it is time to eat a four-course dinner is when the majority of them have said to each other after the cocktail hour, "I'm stuffed."

Let me put it this way. You know how after a satisfying meal, when the waiter asks if you would like to see the dessert menu, you burp and respond, "Thanks, but I couldn't eat another thing." At the wedding, that is the signal to sit down for dinner.

It is not only that the food is so costly. It is that it is so unnecessary. At the moment, most guests would prefer a short nap to a hot appetizer.

As a good host, you have provided your guests with cocktail hour choices that run the gamut from expensive to exorbitant. That is not a wide range. And here are some of the reasons you are getting screwed. A little finger's worth of mackerel, placed on the top of a few grains of white rice, will set you back about as much as a caviar appetizer in a three star Michelin restaurant. Because it is no longer simply raw fish and rice—it is sushi!

Jay H. Heyman

There is another tell tale signal that you are in trouble. The food that you pay for to be served during the cocktail hour will be named *hors d'ouevres*. That final "s" might just as well be a "$." The truth is that translated to English, *hors* means "outside." And *d'ouevre* means "work." Way back when, the miniature appetizers and tidbits served before the main courses were not considered to be particularly difficult to prepare. But in many restaurants today, and certainly the one you are paying for, the thinking was that without adding a final "s" it appeared that you were only serving one appetizer. So even though *hors d'ouevre* means outside of work, you will have to serve — and pay for — *hors d'ouevres*, which roughly translates as "outside of works." A costly grammar lesson.

The good thing is that no matter what entrée choice your guests have decided on,

And I Have to Pay for the F*cking Flowers?

they all will have cost you the same amount. The unfortunate part is that your guest's selections were made weeks ago, early in the day, on an empty stomach, when a nice rib eye with bordelaise sauce and double scooped potatoes seemed very appealing. At the actual moment though, when the waiter asks which main course they wanted, suddenly there is a preponderance of vegetarian platters being requested. If the venue were really clever, they would serve Tums as a side dish, instead of green beans.

There is, actually, one exception to all the entrees costing the same. The exception is whatever the latest food trend is. Currently, the magic word is vegan. Different (more expensive) than vegetarian, it represents still another step in the removal of enjoyment and flavor at the dining table. Those who are vegans choose to avoid any food that had a mother, grew in the ground, has to be peeled, has a pit, has a color that clashes with the napkins, swims, paddles, rows or has a tail, scales, ears or udders.

Perhaps you have decided to beat the system, ignore your daughter's tears, and go the buffet route. Nice try. You will discover that financially, despite all logic, exchanging waiter service for self-service does nothing to lower the price. While at the same time, it will create more unruly crowds than scrambling for the last empty seat in musical chairs.

A buffet is where you can get a really direct insight into your family and guests. Every adult knows that at a buffet, by definition, you can eat as much as you want, returning to the food as often as you wish. But out of some deep-rooted fear of scarcity, there will be guests who will load their plate as if they were auditioning for a spot on "America's Next Top Juggler." They will not

And I Have to Pay for the F*cking Flowers?

care if the beets bleed into the ice cream, or the broccoli into the chocolate tart. They just have this gut feeling that there will soon be armed security guards refusing access to the buffet unless you know the password, which was not included in their invitation.

Jay H. Heyman

A penguin is an expensive role model.

While you may choose to allow your guests to be comfortably and informally attired, you and your wedding party have to be role models. And the role you will be playing is Jay Gatsby. So you will either buy or rent formal wear. But while you believed that a tuxedo usually looked like, well, a tuxedo, you are going to find out that there are variations and customizing options you never would have imagined. Cummerbund? Silk lapel? Pocket square? Patent leather shoes? One-inch cuffs?

Again, you have two choices, neither of which will actually save you any money. You can either rent, or you can decide to purchase the formal wear. Buying, of course, is the most economical option, if you believe that you will be attending future functions that require black tie. That way, the outrageous cost of the outfit can be shared over several outings. But, in the newest definition of irony, the fates have already decided that you will only receive future black tie invitations if you have decided to rent rather than buy.

Renting turns out to be more like leasing. Hidden costs, confrontational negotiations, and time pressures; these all add up to expensive surprises.

Whether you choose to rent or to buy, you have an additional choice; brick and mortar store or online. If you go the in-person route, you will have the added enjoyment of fending off the salesman's efforts to outfit you as if for a royal wedding.

But the real excitement is ordering online. They will have a form that asks more personal questions than a CIA application, and though your third grade teacher's height seems irrelevant, they still would like to know. Also, measuring from top to bottom of this, and side-to-side of that sounds easy, but unless you are an orthopedic surgeon do you really know exactly where your waist is? And do you want your trousers to sit above, at, or below this imaginary horizontal line?

And after you have filled it all out and hit "send" there is the unmatched joy of tensely wondering, as the days tick down, if the tuxedo will arrive in time, if it will fit properly, and that nothing will be missing.

But purchased, rented or bespoke, by the end of the evening the jacket will be ruined, the tie lost, and the shirt shredded.

And I Have to Pay for the F*cking Flowers?

You will lose twenty pounds. Mostly from your wallet.

You have promised yourself to look as trim and fit as you can, since there will be photographic evidence of every excess pound for future generations to chuckle at. But the fact that you will be deceased for most of this future, and therefore will not really care what is being said, will have no effect on your current ego, which also, since it is an ego, refuses to believe you will ever actually die.

The amazing thing is that there is no formula for losing weight. You would think that T+I=PR (time plus incentive equals positive results). You would be wrong. The reality is that the longer ahead you plan, the worse off you will be. Given let's say, four months to prepare, you will spend the first three months saying to yourself, "Oh, I have plenty of time left."

Then comes the final month before the wedding. That's when you realize (rationalize) that if you were to actually lose weight, nothing you have been measured for will now fit properly.

But let's imagine that you are one of the few FOBs who really want to trim down. You might decide to go to your gym more often, except that it's been so long since your last visit, you are no longer sure of the address. Or even if it is still open.

Then somebody, who immediately moves down to the "don't invite" list, mentions Personal Trainers. And even worse, reminds

And I Have to Pay for the F*cking Flowers?

you that they will actually come to your home, which eliminates many of the excuses you have already prepared. But just as your wife will not let a cleaning person into your home until she has done a thorough cleaning—so as not to be embarrassed—you won't let a trainer see what shape you are in until you are in better shape. (This is known in some medical circles as "The dumbass paradox.")

There are many diets from which to choose (Weight Watchers, Jenny Craig, Federal Prison, etc.). And a multitude of plans that promise weight loss if just one item is eliminated; fats, sugars, carbohydrates, anything colored mauve, and so on. Traditionally, we are told that these should not be referred to as "diets," because that indicates a time-limited change of eating habits. Instead, they should be regarded as simply a modification of your nutritional lifestyle, indicating a lifetime commitment to hunger pangs.

And just as wedding customs go in and out of fashion, so too do diets. However, the core evolution in the rules of dieting seems to be simply the substitution of "Always" for "Never." As in the change of "Never eat a cucumber without peeling it," to "Always eat a cucumber without peeling it."

The central evolution in wedding customs, however, is always monetary, and never to your financial benefit.

And I Have to Pay for the F*cking Flowers?

The Cake. It's spelled "tiers," but it's pronounced "tears."

Marie-Antoinette famously proclaimed, "Let them eat cake." Because even then she somehow knew that you were going to pay for it.

This will be an easy one for you to beat, you think. You are planning on simply bringing in your own desserts.

Nope.

Again, using wedding economic logic, it will cost you more to bring in your own dessert than to have the hall serve their own. This is due to an economic theory, which you may have heard of before, known as, "Because we can." Which explains why you are crying.

The problem is that the cake is largely symbolic. You certainly don't want to actually eat the cake—or anything else—since you are still filled up from the cocktail hour, the meal, and the cookies and sweets that were placed on each table. But you will have to order a cake. And it will have more layers than the maid of honor's hairdo, be taller than the bride and weigh more than the groom. As a further example of how most of your money is wasted, its main function is to have the happy couple slice a piece and feed it to each other. So there will now be a cherished memory of the couple's messy, sloppy faces, covered with cake and whipped cream. There may never be a time when they will be more happy, or look more silly.

And I Have to Pay for the F*cking Flowers?

The cake will then be sliced by a (highly) paid professional, and served to each guest. Along with their choice of coffees, and twelve different teas, ranging in name from evening orange blend to chamomile. And not surprisingly, by this time of the evening, each tea, no matter the fancy description, will taste exactly like the mini porcelain teacups with no handles served in Chinese restaurants, that, when they are cool enough to handle, are too cold to enjoy. Plus those little packets of artificial sweeteners, each a different color. And each color with its own individual history of being blamed for medical issues with various organs.

Jay H. Heyman

No matter what your favorite flowers are, they will be out of season.

When we are talking the expense of flowers, you have to understand that they are the textbook perfecta: nothing else at a wedding costs more and has a shorter lifespan.

Bouquets for the bridal party. Boutonnieres. Arrangements to distribute around the ceremony area. Table vases. That's just to mention of few of the opportunities you will have to outshine your local department store's annual flower show budget. And while the store may have community sponsors, all you have are allergies and a new respect for your

And I Have to Pay for the F*cking Flowers?

neighborhood's homeless population, who never anticipated ending up penniless either.

My personal favorites are the table vases. Though each size will cost the same, you will have to decide if you prefer the smaller height, so that the closeness of the flowers' aroma can overpower the food, or select the higher size, so that visibility of the other guests at the table is mostly blocked.

What flowers will you put in the vases? Though you can plan as you wish, you will end up with out of season, botanical garden, blue-ribbon worthy specimens imported from Japan or Italy. And if what you had in mind were roses and daffodils, you hopefully won't mind when they become ranunculus, oncidium orchid, lisianthus, and hellebore. And don't worry about the spelling. The common name for each of them is Ka-Ching! Hell, you will find that what you once considered weeds are now considered exotica. Still, let's admit that the bouquets will be gorgeous, with beautiful colors and stunning arrangements. Which is why you will once again be puzzled when the florist spray paints the flowers so that they all are the same arbitrary color that has been selected by "them."

Incidentally, it never ends.

I am calling them the "incidentals." These are the assortment of smallish items that you don't really pay much attention to, because you assume they must be inexpensive. Well, the sad fact that for the FOB, nothing is inexpensive. These so-called incidentals will end up costing you an arm and a leg, if you haven't already used these limbs for previous purchases.

Yarmulkes. These are the little skullcaps worn at Jewish weddings, designed by elderly rabbis in ancient times to cover the bald spot at the top of their heads. No matter how progressive or liberal the affair, tradition dictates that there be one available for every male guest. Then come the color and fabric choices; each choice, of course, priced separately. Finally, add the cost of the names inscribed inside the caps, placed there so that people in the future can wonder who the hell were Shawn and Sage, and were we actually at their wedding? Realistically, only one in twenty yarmulkes will make it out of the venue alive. The rest will be left under the tables or on the dance floor, and sacrilegiously swept up at the end of the festivities. But worn, discarded, taken as souvenirs or lost in the tumult, you will pay for each and every one.

Transportation. You may have heard of "Last mile delivery." This is the term used for the final delivery of goods from a major retail or online store. Like when goods are shipped cross-country, and then FedEx puts

And I Have to Pay for the F*cking Flowers?

it on one of its trucks for the last part of the journey to your home.

Similarly, "Transportation" in this sense does not mean getting guests from their home to the hotel that has been booked. That is, hopefully, not your problem (expense). But you are going to be on the hook for getting the guests from the hotel to the venue and back. Depending on the distance and what city you are in, this could be, for example, a taxi, bus, a stroll, Uber, or horse-drawn carriage.

But it won't be.

You will be providing your guests with limousine service, no matter how pleasant the weather is, how close the hotel is to the destination, and in what great shape your guests are in. If you have to ask why you are burdened by this unnecessary expenditure, you have not been reading this guide carefully enough. Or, if you would like a lesson in classic double talk, ask "them."

The after party. If you have any sense of humor left, you will chuckle at the use of the word "party" to describe the insane attempt to continue the festivities past all realistic expectations or desire. You will have paid to have a room or bar area remain open late, so that all those who require a nightcap can be accommodated. But just so you know, the money you are paying for this is not really for the bar service; it is for the crucial presence of bathroom attendants, and their wet cloths, towels, and mouthwash.

From the bartender's perspective, there will mainly be a row of heads resting on stretched out arms on the bar. And what he will hear if anyone actually orders a beverage is so unintelligible even Google translate won't stand a chance.

And I Have to Pay for the F*cking Flowers?

But most of this does not really matter, since only about 2 of your guests will actually go to the after party, and half of those were actually just looking for the elevator.

The morning after. In some ways—congratulations—this is the biggest waste of your money. Remember how, when your guests were satiated from the cocktail party, you directed them to the dining room and encouraged them to enjoy a four-course dinner? O.K. Now picture them, after having force-fed themselves dinner like French geese being prepped for their foie gras, and after having consumed insane amounts of alcohol, and been shamed into going to the after party and gotten maybe two hours of sleep, being awakened the next morning and reminded that they had checked 'Yes" to the celebration breakfast. So, bleary of eye, and with their now protruding belly the first part of their body to enter, they stumble into the breakfast room, looking as if they were auditioning for *Zombies at a Wedding*.

Fortunately, they will not remember any of this. Unfortunately, this memory lapse will include the entire wedding ceremony.

And I Have to Pay for the F*cking Flowers?

The venue. So many variables. So much money.

This is the single most important financial wedding decision you will have to make. Hotel? Garden? Rooftop? Home? Restaurant? Country Club? Barge? Brewery? Hostel? Alley? Winery? Tent? Marina?

And since this is one of your first decisions, you will actually have a fleeting sense that you are in control.

Well, as the ancient seers responded when asked about the best crop fertilizer, "Bullshit." Sure, this is an important monetary decision, but you will find out that your planning, pondering, and thoughtful insights don't matter. There will be absolutely no cost savings, no matter what you do. (Have you noticed the pattern?)

But you ask what about, for example, the yacht on the lake that offers an all-inclusive package? You will discover that the definition of an all-inclusive, as it pertains to a wedding, is that an all-inclusive includes all the things that it includes. But it does not include all the things that it does not include. This is where you will first experience the magic and tragedy of the asterisk. It looks like a small thing (it looks like this: *). But it will invade your 401k as mercilessly as boll weevils at a cotton festival.

All the items you are likely to believe are included, because they seem so basic, such as chairs, candles, coat check, bathroom attendant and valet, will each have a tiny asterisk attached to them. And at the bottom

And I Have to Pay for the F*cking Flowers?

of the page will be the answering asterisk, with these two deadly words attached: *Not Included.

Keep in mind, the larger the venue, the more guests you can invite. And the more guests you invite, the more money....oh, you figured that one out already.

I have hesitated to mention the biggest venue money vacuum of all, since if you have read this far, I do not know if that is your normal heart rate. This is the destination wedding. If you love irony, you will love the idea that no matter where you live, you may travel somewhere else for the actual nuptials. What makes this so classically ironic are the high odds that the wedding party who live near your wedding destination will be coming to your hometown for *their* destination wedding.

Jay H. Heyman

Help! There are so many of "them," and only one of me.

Yes, you are vastly outnumbered. And probably will be really fucked. But do you remember David and Goliath? He was just one little guy against a humongous giant, and according to legend, he persevered. And while it is true that there was only one giant, not the hordes aligned against you, somehow this is meant to cheer you up.

So what can I do to help? Here are a few thoughts that may ease your financial pain. But keep in mind this will be at the risk of alienating your daughter, your wife, your future son-in-law and even your next door

And I Have to Pay for the F*cking Flowers?

neighbor's cousin, whom you are forced to invite because you want to continue to use your neighbor's pool, but who somehow will hear about why he was really invited and either not send a wedding gift, or worse, send another grotesque silver plated picture frame.

- Tell your daughter the exact amount you are prepared to provide for the wedding. It should be the actual total you are comfortable with, and you have to stick to it, no matter how her eyes well up when she realizes that you are serious and not doing another daddy practical joke.

- Spend lavishly and go crazy, but right before the final checks are due, go into Chapter 7 bankruptcy, so you can lose your pride, but still keep your house.

Jay H. Heyman

- Go into your very own witness protection program. Change your name, move to another state, and grow/remove any facial hair. This way, you can still attend the wedding, though you will have to be introduced as your own long lost uncle.

- Buy lottery tickets. Lots and lots of lottery tickets.

- Get on a TV quiz show, and win tons of money. This only works if you actually are smart enough to know the answers. And since you have already purchased a book like this, the odds are not in your favor.

- Write your own book about how screwed the FOB is, though the jury is still out as to whether or not writing this guide has been the financial Fort Knox I had hoped for.

And I Have to Pay for the F*cking Flowers?

Have you noticed a theme here?

At some point, someone will suggest that instead of random bits and pieces, wouldn't it be cool if you tied everything together? The real answer is, how the hell should you know?

The real, real answer is, cool or not, it will cost more to have a theme. So of course you will end up having one. While you may prefer a realistic theme such as debtor's prison, or a Dickensian workhouse, "they" will insist on something more glamorous.

The theme might be a color, a location, a phrase, a date, or a special event, but upscale it will be. And since everything must fit into this theme, forced or not, your wallet will once again feel major pangs of hunger as it is once more being emptied.

By this point, it should not surprise you to know that no matter what theme is selected, there will be nothing ready made that fits it. If the theme is based on colors, for example, "their" selection will be the only shade that does not have a matching Pantone equivalent. So it all must be customized. And have you ever found a custom anything that costs less than the off the rack version? Everything, from the napkins to the balloons, must match precisely, or there will be hell to pay — and you know who will be paying the hell.

However, let's say the theme is not based on a color or color combination. Maybe it's a simple theme, such as the couple's name. But as you breathe your sigh of relief, take

And I Have to Pay for the F*cking Flowers?

another deep breath. Because it is about to get very personal. As in the enchanting phrase, "personalized." Yes, it is hard to imagine why this is necessary. Everyone at the wedding knows the names of the couple that is getting married. But to insure there is no misunderstanding, their names are engraved, glued or etched onto every empty surface. And no matter how few surfaces you think there could be, you are way off. Though you may think that aside from luggage tags, where else does it make sense to inscribe a name, you will discover just how many different items can be personalized. Whether they should be is another matter. For example, names will appear on cake toppers, napkins, banners, cake bags, champagne flutes, gift bags, tote bags, water bottle labels, and votive holders, to mention just the obvious surfaces.

Jay H. Heyman

Of course, if there were truly concerns that no one would know the wedding couple's names, the easiest solution would simply be to have the bride and groom wear nametags. But then the theme would turn into, "Are you kidding me?"

OK, I know the groom goes through some shit too.

Though it doesn't in any meaningful way compare to the pain you feel as the FOB, the groom does have one or two monetary aches. His main problem is that an engagement ring is seemingly the only sufficient proof of a groom's honorable intentions. Of course, it has to be a diamond ring! And of course, it can't just be an ordinary diamond ring.

It must outshine in every one of the 4Cs categories. (Color. Clarity. Cut. Carat.)

Jay H. Heyman

Now, stepping back, we realize that we are talking about a hunk of coal. Basically the same stuff you light bags of to grill your steak. But let a few billion years or so pass, and suddenly it turns into a shiny object designed to do one thing—piss off the bridesmaids.

Of course, there are synthetic diamonds—artificial, if you will—that look, to the untrained, normal, 20-20 eyes, to be identical to the high priced charcoal version. But a jeweler will be delighted to take out his 10x loupe and show you that deep inside there may be a dot of difference. When the groom points out that most of his friends don't usually carry a magnifying glass, he gets the same pitying glare in response that you expect from a funeral director when he learns that you don't want to purchase the mahogany, brass ringed, silk-lined casket.

And I Have to Pay for the F*cking Flowers?

Remember, as much as jewelers talk up the 4Cs, they omit the most important C: **Cost**! This is actually the most essential difference between the real thing and the seemingly not real thing. But who is to say? Gold is worth whatever gold is worth because people say that that is what it is worth. Same for diamonds.

And speaking of gold, which often happens when the discussion concerns weddings, after the groom buys this knockout, showy, gleaming diamond, he is then expected to minimize its glory. For he then has to purchase a shiny gold band to put on his bride's finger next to the diamond ring, to detract from the ring's splendor. And this outlay for gold and diamonds is all done fully realizing that half the marriages in America end in divorce. The other half ends in silence.

Which leads to the other predicament for the groom. The pre-nuptial agreement. A pre-nuptial agreement is intended to make it easier, should (when) the marriage not endure. It allocates the assets of the couple in an orderly, pre-arranged manner. And though it may cost a pretty penny to set up, it beats the ugly penny that it would cost not to have this in place. There is only one difficulty. It comes at the moment the future groom looks adoringly at his soon to be spouse and tenderly asks her "to love, honor, obey…and sign here."

And I Have to Pay for the F*cking Flowers?

The good news.

Jay H. Heyman

About The Author

The husband of one and the father of two, Jay lives in Manhattan, in the formerly fashionable Upper East Side.

Jay is a founder and creative director of a New York advertising agency, which recently celebrated its 25th anniversary. During his advertising career, Jay has written ads for Skippy Peanut Butter, Trix, Total and Cocoa Puffs cereals, The Curacao Tourist Board, Anacin, Fruit Stripe Gum, Old Spice Deodorant, and Dallas BBQ restaurants, among many others.

Having recently walked his daughter down the aisle, Jay has experienced the bliss of realizing that he is no longer responsible for paying for the straightening of her teeth, or the curling of her hair.

And I Have to Pay for the F*cking Flowers?

This short walk down the aisle—which on a cost per foot basis is more expensive than an Uber at full "It's Saturday night and it's raining" surge pricing—has led directly to his creation of this guide.

However, unlike a movie that proudly proclaims it is based on true events, this guide is completely fictional, and has little to do with his own time as an FOB.

You can reach him on Twitter @uneedagoodidea.

100 per cent of the profits from the sale of this book will go toward paying off some of his outstanding wedding bills.

P.S. Thank you for taking the time to read my book. If you smiled, giggled, or guffawed I have done my job. If you actually peed your pants, I have exceeded my goal. I do have one request; please leave a review. If you didn't like it, that's fine too. Just leave an honest review.

And if you are truly an FOB, congratulations; no matter what it all cost, you know it is more than worth it.

Made in the USA
Middletown, DE
30 July 2018